WITHDRAWN

EXPLORING WORLD CULTURES

United Kingdom

Gemma Greig

Cavendish
Square

New York

Published in 2018 by Cavendish Square Publishing, LLC
243 5th Avenue, Suite 136, New York, NY 10016

Copyright © 2018 by Cavendish Square Publishing, LLC

First Edition

Library of Congress Cataloging-in-Publication Data

Names: Greig, Gemma, author.
Title: United Kingdom / Gemma Greig.
Description: New York : Cavendish Square Publishing, 2018. |
Series: Exploring world cultures | Includes index.
Identifiers: LCCN 2017021707 (print) | LCCN 2017022196 (ebook) |
ISBN 9781502630346 (E-book) | ISBN 9781502630315 (pbk.) | ISBN 9781502630322 (6 pack) |
ISBN 9781502630339 (library bound)
Subjects: LCSH: Great Britain--Juvenile literature.
Classification: LCC DA27.5 (ebook) | LCC DA27.5 .G75 2018 (print) |
DDC 941--dc23
LC record available at https://lccn.loc.gov/2017021707

Editorial Director: David McNamara
Editor: Kristen Susienka
Copy Editor: Alex Tessman
Associate Art Director: Amy Greenan
Designer: Graham Abbott
Production Coordinator: Karol Szymczuk
Photo Research: J8 Media

Printed in the United States of America

Contents

Introduction

The United Kingdom has many different people living in it. It is made up of four other countries: Wales, Scotland, England, and Northern Ireland. It has over 2.5 million years of history.

Many other countries and cultures have made the United Kingdom what it is today. The Romans brought roads to the United Kingdom, and the French helped to shape the English language.

Today the United Kingdom has modern and old buildings. Roads, railroads, and airports make it easy to travel around the United Kingdom and to other countries. Many people live in the United

Kingdom, speak different languages, and share different customs. The United Kingdom is an exciting place to live in and explore.

This is a busy shopping street in Leeds, England. You can see many old buildings and modern shops.

The United Kingdom is
a country in Europe. It
is made up of England,
Wales, Scotland, and
Northern Ireland. Its
total size is 94,058
square miles (243,610
square kilometers). Its
only land border is with

A map of the United Kindom

the Republic of Ireland. The sea surrounds it on
all other sides. The highest point is a mountain

The United Kingdom is almost twice the
size of the state of New York.

in Scotland called Ben Nevis. It is 4,406 feet (1,343 meters) high.

The beautiful hills and valleys of Glencoe, Scotland

England is the most crowded of the four countries in the United Kingdom. There are lots of cities and towns in Northern Ireland, Scotland, and Wales. They also have a lot of countryside. Each country in the United Kingdom has its own capital city, soccer (called football) team, and **parliament**.

The River Thames

The most famous river in the United Kingdom is the River Thames. It flows through England's capital city, London.

The United Kingdom has a long history. The first people arrived there over 2.5 million years ago. These people formed groups called tribes. They used stones as tools and weapons.

London's Buckingham Palace shines in the sun. This is where the king or queen lives.

In 55 CE, a group called the Romans invaded the United Kingdom. They made huge changes, like building roads. Later, a family called the Tudors ruled from 1485 CE to 1603 CE. In 1603, the ruler, Queen Elizabeth I, died. She did not have

Henry the Eighth

One of the United Kingdom's most well-known kings was Henry VIII. He had six wives and beheaded two of them.

King Henry VIII of England is known for his many wives.

a child to take over, so the throne was passed on to Scottish cousins. They were called the Stuarts. Then it went to the Georgians, the Victorians, and finally to the Windsors. The Windsors still rule the country today.

FACT!

The ruins of Roman roads and buildings can still be found all over the United Kingdom.

The United Kingdom has a parliament and a **monarchy**. The ruler is a king or a queen. Today, the queen attends many ceremonies but does not have a lot of power in the government. The head of parliament is called the prime minister.

Queen Elizabeth II and her husband, the Duke of Edinburgh, wave to a crowd.

Parliament is located in London, England. Officials called Members of Parliament help make laws for England and for the United Kingdom. The parliament in London makes big decisions that

Two Sides

Parliament has two parts, or houses. They are called the House of Lords and the House of Commons.

The House of Parliament in London

all countries in the United Kingdom must follow. Wales, Scotland, and Northern Ireland have their own parliaments in their capital cities that make other decisions that each person in that country must follow.

FACT!

UK citizens vote for a Member of Parliament in a general election. The party with the most Members of Parliament in the House of Commons leads the government and the leader of the party becomes the prime minister.

The Economy

Today, the United Kingdom has one of the strongest **economies** in the world. The cities of Edinburgh, Scotland, and London, England, are two of the largest financial centers in Europe.

Pounds are colorful. Here are shown £5, £10, and £50 bills, or banknotes.

In the past, the United Kingdom's most popular industry was manufacturing. Many ships and planes were built in the country before and during World War I and World War II. The United Kingdom also makes cars, train equipment, and electronics.

Tourism

Tourism makes up a huge part of the United Kingdom's economy. London is the second-most-visited city in the world.

Today, many different industries make up the economy. Tourism, banking, and oil production are big industries for the United Kingdom. The United Kingdom also grows a lot of

Businessmen walk to work in London.

food, like grains and potatoes, and raises cows and sheep.

FACT!

The United Kingdom's currency is called the pound sterling, or the pound. It it is the world's oldest and longest-running currency.

The environment is important in the United Kingdom. There are forests, grassy areas, farmland, and cities. Birds, cows, sheep, and horses are popular animals in the countryside. There are also animals that live in forests. Deer and elk are common in the Scottish Highlands.

Pine Martins are a protected species in the United Kingdom.

Recycling is an important part of life in the United Kingdom. Homes have recycling bins that are collected once a week or once every two weeks.

The warmest months of the year in the United Kingdom are July and August.

Cities also have areas where people can throw away garbage or recycling.

The United Kingdom has warm summers and cool winters. The summers do not get as hot as countries in Europe, and winters do not get as cold. It does rain a lot in some parts of the country. The United Kingdom also has beaches.

Lots of Land

In England, only 2.27 percent of the landscape is considered to be "built on."

People enjoy a day at the beach in Kent, England.

There are many different people living in the United Kingdom. Altogether, the country has a population of sixty-four million people. Some people were born there. Other

London has many tourists, shoppers, and commuters every day.

Manners

UK citizens believe in good manners. It is important to say "please" and "thank you." It is also polite when visiting someone's house to bring a small gift. Examples could be cookies or flowers.

people came to the United Kingdom from different countries. People bring many different cultures and traditions to the United Kingdom. Because the country has a mix of cultures, citizens can be any race, culture, or religion.

People living in the United Kingdom can call themselves English, Scottish, Welsh, or Irish. People living in the four countries have different traditions but share similarities. Many people enjoy going to the pub to socialize, listening to upbeat music, and hill walking.

FACT!

London has the biggest population in the United Kingdom with 8.6 million people.

There are many different lifestyles in the United Kingdom. Some people work in cities. Others are farmers. Some people are businesspeople, teachers, or doctors. Others work in factories.

A traditional Scottish wedding has people dressed in tartan, called plaid in the United States.

Today, many people wait until they are older to get married and have children. Many people focus on careers first and have families later. The average age to get married is thirty for a woman and thirty-two for a man. There has also been a rise in single-parent families

Women in the UK

It is illegal in the United Kingdom to discriminate against somebody because she is a woman.

in the UK as well as **civil partnerships** since they were introduced in 2004.

Many people live in apartments, called flats. There are more people living in houses, too. In the countryside, people live on farms. Some people live in villages outside cities.

A family enjoys an evening meal together at home. Many families eat dinner at home. Sometimes they might go out to eat, too.

The average number of people living as a family in one household in the United Kingdom is 2.4.

19

Religion

Everyone living in the United Kingdom has the right to choose their religion. All people try to respect other people's religious beliefs.

According to a **census** in 2011, the United Kingdom's largest

Muslim men praying at a mosque in London.

religion is Christianity. Its second-largest religion is Islam, followed by Hinduism, Sikhism, Judaism, and Buddhism.

FACT!

The king or queen of the United Kingdom has to be a Protestant.

20

Although the United Kingdom does not have an official religion, historically it has been a Christian country. Today there are two branches of Christianity in the United Kingdom: Roman Catholic and Protestant. Most Christians in the United Kingdom are Protestant. Many belong to either the Church of England or the Church of Scotland. The head of the Church of England is the king or queen.

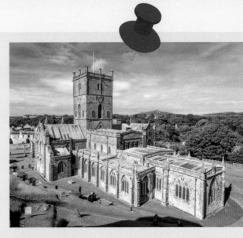

Saint David's Cathedral in Wales was built in 1180 CE. It is thought to be the fourth structure built on this land.

To Worship or Not

Many people in the United Kingdom do not practice any religion at all. As of 2010, 28 percent of the population did not have a religion.

Language

The main language spoken in the United Kingdom is British English. This is slightly different from American English. British English spells words differently than American English. Some words are also different. For example, a person in the United Kingdom would say "rubbish" instead of "garbage."

A road sign appears in both English (*top*) and Welsh (*bottom*).

FACT!

There is thought to be around one hundred different languages spoken in the United Kingdom.

Many Languages

There are different languages even among the **British Isles.** For example, Cornish is spoken in Cornwall, Manx in the Isle of Man, and Shelta in Ireland.

Some Welsh people speak Welsh; someone living in areas of Scotland speaks a language called Gaelic (GAL-IK). There are many different English accents in the United Kingdom, too. Somebody from London will have a different accent to someone from Newcastle or Glasgow. Visitors to some of these regions might find the different accents difficult to understand, even if the visitor speaks English very well.

Arts and Festivals

People in the United Kingdom enjoy arts and festivals. The United Kingdom has many art galleries and places to see plays or musicals.

Different towns and cities have different festivals and celebrations. Traditional Christian holidays are observed, like Christmas and Easter. In the summer, many

The Royal Mile, a famous road in Edinburgh, Scotland, hosts the Edinburgh Fringe Festival.

Creative people in the United Kingdom are supported by organizations like the Arts Council England.

nonreligious festivals happen. Some are music festivals, dance festivals, or book festivals. The Edinburgh Fringe Festival in Scotland is held every August. It attracts performers and theater companies from all over the world. Many tourists visit the United Kingdom during this time to see the festivals.

Europe's biggest carnival also happens in August in London. It is called the Notting Hill Carnival. The streets of West London are taken over by Caribbean music, food, and dance.

April Fool's

On April Fool's Day, people in the United Kingdom play tricks on each other, but only before noon, or the joke is on you.

People in the United Kingdom enjoy sports. Cricket is the national sport of England. Soccer, called football there, is the most popular sport. It is played by most kids at school. Other common sports played in

England (*white*) plays Ireland (*green*) in a rugby match.

the United Kingdom are tennis, golf, and rugby. England, Scotland, Wales, and Northern Ireland have their own football and rugby teams and will

In the United Kingdom, people spend about twenty-five hours a week watching television.

often play against each other in big tournaments.

The most common pastime for people of the United Kingdom is watching television. There are many TV channels and shows to watch.

A group of children play "football," or soccer.

Other leisure activities include going to the cinema, listening to music, going to concerts, and spending time with friends and family.

Weekends

Weekends (Saturdays and Sundays) are popular days in the United Kingdom. Saturday is usually a busy shopping day. Sundays are days of rest.

27

Food

Food in the United Kingdom is often inspired by meals from other cultures. As people move to the United Kingdom, they bring their traditions and recipes with them. The city of Birmingham is thought to be the curry capital of the United Kingdom. However, the first takeout food in the United Kingdom was fish and chips in 1860.

The town Melton Mowbray produces a traditional English pork pie. A pork pie is chopped pork meat and pastry with jelly separating the two.

Many different pork pies are on sale at a market stall in Manchester, England.

28

A Pork Pie Appreciation Society meets once a week to taste pork pies and rate their taste.

A soft drink called Irn Bru is popular in Scotland. Scottish people buy more Irn Bru than Coca-Cola, and the recipe for Irn Bru is a secret. A dish called toad in the hole is another traditional UK dish.

A can of Irn Bru. It is Scotland's popular and colorful soft drink.

English Breakfast

An English breakfast is a meal of eggs, sausage, bacon, grilled tomato, beans, and toast.

Glossary

British Isles   A group of islands. Making up the British Isles are the United Kingdom, Ireland, and smaller islands belonging to the countries.

census   A list of questions used to get information. Each question asks about a different part of life in a country. A census is given every ten years.

civil partnerships   Legal recognition of a relationship between same-sex couples.

economy   A system of goods or services that helps make a country successful.

monarchy   A government with a king or a queen.

parliament   The name of a group of people that represent and make decisions for a country's citizens.

Find Out More

Books

Combe, Carey, Sara Harper, et al., eds. *Eyewitness Travel Guide to London*. New York: DK Publishers, 2016.

Hall, Geoff, and Kamila Kasperowicz. *British Stuff: Life in Britain Through 101 Everyday Objects*. Chichester, UK: Summersdale Publishers Ltd, 2013.

Website

Project Britain

http://projectbritain.com

Video

Top Ten Facts about the UK

https://www.youtube.com/watch?v=Jrka9Nt-nQo

Learn more about the United Kingdom in this short, fun video.

Index

About the Author

Gemma Greig was born and raised in Scotland. Today she is an editor for a publishing company in Bristol, England. She studied at Edinburgh Napier University and moved to Bristol after graduation in 2012. She enjoys writing, reading, and traveling the world.